us

HYACINTH,
the Reluctant Duck

By Ann Tompert

Illustrated by John Paul Richards

Steck-Vaughn Company • Austin, Texas

An Intext Publisher

ISBN 0-8114-7740-1
Library of Congress Catalog Card Number 76-176071
Copyright © 1972 by Steck-Vaughn Company, Austin, Texas

Crack! From an egg in an incubator,
a little duckling suddenly appeared.

Jerry called her "Hyacinth."

She had no mother or father or
brothers or sisters.

4

Hyacinth followed Jerry's dog
Nelson everywhere. The little
duckling did not know she was a
duck. She thought she was a dog.

Hyacinth tried to do everything
Nelson did.

She turned up her bill at the
wheat Jerry gave her. She would
not eat the cracked corn. She
waddled away when Jerry offered
her bugs and worms. Instead, she
ate Nelson's dog food.

When Jerry placed Hyacinth in
a little pool to swim, she set up a
dreadful squawking and flounced off
to a far corner of the yard.

Nelson took long drinks of water
from the pool.

After Hyacinth saw this, she
circled the pool several times.
Then she, too, took a drink from it.

From that time on, both the dog and
the duckling used the little pool as
their water dish.

Hyacinth had her own house with a
bed of straw, but she would not use it.
Instead, she slept every night beside
Nelson in his doghouse.

Nelson liked to stand at the back
gate and speak to everyone who passed.
"Bow-wow! Bow-wow!" he barked.

Hyacinth wanted to talk to people, too, but she didn't quack like a duck or bark like a dog. "Back! Wack! Back! Wack!" Hyacinth squawked.

Every day, Nelson ran to pick up
the newspaper. He carried it to
Jerry's father.

Jerry's father patted Nelson on the
head. "Good dog! Good dog!" he said.

One day, Hyacinth got the newspaper
and hurried to find Jerry's father.
But she couldn't hold the newspaper in
her flat bill.

A gust of wind came along and
scattered paper all over the front
yard and down the street. But this
did not discourage Hyacinth from
trying to be a dog.

The next day, Nelson chased a brown
cat up a tree.

Hyacinth waited until the brown cat
came down. "Back! Wack! Back!
Wack!" she squawked. Then she charged
at the cat.

But the cat did not run. Instead, she arched her back and slapped Hyacinth.

Hyacinth flew to the safety of the doghouse.

A few days later, Nelson dug a deep hole. He wanted to hide a bone.

Hyacinth found a stick and began to scratch the ground beside the hole Nelson had dug.

But the little duckling couldn't make
her feet go the right way. She tumbled
into the hole Nelson had dug.

"Back! Wack!" wailed Hyacinth.
She scrambled out of the hole as fast
as she could.

Then one day, Hyacinth laid an egg.
She ran around in circles all afternoon.
How upset she was! Hyacinth knew that
Nelson had never laid an egg.

She tried to hide the egg under a
bush. Then she huddled in a far corner
of the yard and refused to eat anything.

"It is time Hyacinth learned she is a
duck, not a dog," said Jerry's father.

The next afternoon they all drove
to Grandfather's farm.

As soon as they arrived, Nelson raced
to the pond where Grandfather's ducks
were swimming. Into the water he plunged
with great splashes.

Hyacinth waddled to the pond, but she just stood at the edge of the water.

"Quack! Quack! Quack!" called Grandfather's ducks.

"Quack! Quack! Quack!" answered
Hyacinth, surprised at the sound she
was making. She tumbled into the pond.

The duckling flapped her wings.
Her feet moved this way and that.
But soon she was gliding gracefully
over the water toward the other ducks.

Hyacinth stayed with her new friends
all afternoon. When it was time to go
home, she swam toward Jerry.

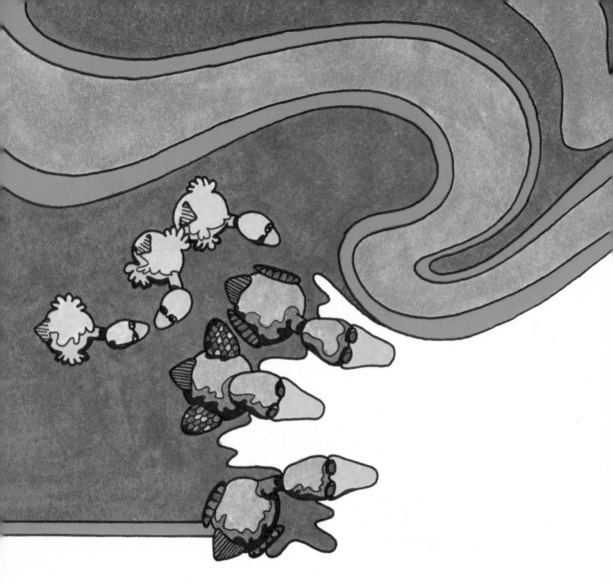

"Quack! Quack!" called the other ducks.
Hyacinth circled back toward them.

Jerry called and Nelson barked. Once
more, Hyacinth started to swim toward
the bank.

"Quack! Quack!" the ducks called after her.

Hyacinth circled back to the ducks again.

Jerry called and called. Nelson
barked and barked. But this time
Hyacinth stayed with the other ducks.

"Hyacinth will be happier if she
stays with my ducks," said Grandfather.

Jerry thought and thought. He looked back at Hyacinth swimming in the pond with the other ducks. "Yes," he agreed, "but I will miss her. Nelson will, too."

Jerry sighed. "She will probably forget all about us."

Hyacinth did not forget, however. Every
time Jerry and Nelson visited Grandfather,
out from the flock of ducks waddled one
special duck. It was Hyacinth greeting
them with a happy "Back! Wack! Back!
Wack!"